For my dear ones, Juliette and Sébastien.
All my gratitude to Elsa M., Anne-Caroline, Céline C., Jean-François,
Bénédicte, Domitille, Cédric, Lize, Claudine, Thomas, Céline O.,
Olivia G., Aude, Clémentine, Aurélie de H., Yun Jung, Olivia B.,
my parents, Marion, Laurent, Camille, Sandrine, Catherine F., André,
and Aurélie C., who all brought precious branches to my fort!

THIS IS A NEW YORK REVIEW BOOK
PUBLISHED BY THE NEW YORK REVIEW OF BOOKS
435 Hudson Street, New York, NY 10014
www.nyrb.com

Library of Congress Cataloging-in-Publication Data
Names: Dorléans, Marie, author, illustrator. | Waters, Alyson, 1955– translator.
Title: Our fort / by Marie Dorléans ; translated by Alyson Waters.
Other titles: Notre cabane. English
Description: New York : New York Review Books, 2022. | Series: New York Review children's col-
    lection | Summary: Three friends set out to visit their secret fort at the edge of the woods, but
    as they are enjoying the freedom and nature all around them a big storm rolls in.
Identifiers: LCCN 2021027799 | ISBN 9781681376585 (hardcover)
Subjects: CYAC: Nature--Fiction. | Friendship--Fiction.
Classification: LCC PZ7.1.D674 Ou 2022 | DDC [E]—dc23
LC record available at https://lccn.loc.gov/2021027799

ISBN: 978-168137-658-5

Printed in China on acid-free paper.
10   9   8   7   6   5   4   3   2   1

Our Fort

Written and illustrated by
Marie Dorléans

Translated from the French by Alyson Waters

The New York Review Children's Collection
New York

It's spring! Every day, nature calls to us to come outside and play.
Birds chirp in the garden. Trees rustle in the sunlight.
It's as if the entire countryside were waiting impatiently for us to wander through it.
"Hey, guys! Want to go to the fort?"
"Yes! To the fort!"

"See you tonight, Elsa!"
"You'll let me come with you
someday, won't you?"
"As soon as you've learned how
to keep a secret!"
The adventure will begin the
minute we step through the gate.

First, we pass our neighbor's house.
We tend to walk a little faster when we go by.
"Why does the dog bark at us every time?"
"Don't worry, he's on a leash."
"Listen: Even the warblers are afraid to sing now!"

Next, we walk past the sheep meadow. Usually we offer the sheep a few blades of grass through the fence. We each have one of our own. We've named our sheep Titus, Alfred, and Gideon.
But today we have so much to tell each other that we forget to say hi to them.
"I found a little saw in the attic at home. We can bring it with us next time, to make our fort stronger."
"That sounds great, but your parents will never let you take it."
"We'll show them that we know how to use it!"

Vast, billowing green fields stretch out in front of us, as far as the eye can see.
"Should we take a shortcut through the grass?"
"Everyone make your own path!"
"First one there gets twice as many snacks!"

We plow ahead haphazardly, swallowed up by the tall grasses where we love to get lost.

"You win!"
"Wow, I'm so lucky! These are my favorite cookies!"
"Look at that! There are still crumbs here from yesterday.
Seems like the larks aren't crazy about our cookies!"
Every now and then, the shadow of a passing cloud flickers
across the meadow.

"I'll bet no one will be able to find us."
"And we'll have to make a campfire and sleep in the woods."
"And eat grasshoppers, field mice, and mushrooms."
We hear murmurs in the air all around us—vague, distant
whispers, as if the sky were plotting something.

"Look at all these crows! Where could they possibly be going?"
"What did you say? I can hardly hear you!"
"Crows, I said. Crows! It's strange. It seems like they're fleeing something."
Suddenly everything grows dark, and a sound swells and draws near.

"I can't walk forward anymore!"
"Me neither."
"And I can't . . . I can't talk anymore."
The air rushes in from everywhere.
Around us, everything bristles, then goes limp, then rears up again.

Now winds gather from all sides, racing toward us.
"Hold on! Don't let me go!"
"I can't see a thing! Where are you?"
The gusts charge at us, recede, then pick up speed again...

Now the winds howl and swirl.
They surround us, jostle us, and topple us over.
Everything is topsy-turvy; right side up, then
upside down. Day turns to night.
"Where are we?"
Our words are swallowed by the blustery wind.

We hold on with all our might.
We turn into stone statues to brace ourselves.
Little by little, the gusts grow weaker, and softer, and
slowly retreat into the distance.

They leave behind only a tiny whistle of a breeze, a gentle caress.
"I feel like it was all a dream."
"More like a nightmare!"

"Look!"

The countryside slowly recovers.
The sparrows are already singing as the sun returns.
"I was afraid we'd fly away!"
"Like we were as light as a feather!"
"I was soooo scared!"
"Me too. Big time!"
"Do you think our fort is still standing? The storm
must have blown everything away…"

Amazing!
It's been spared. It sits imposingly, intact and proud,
in the middle of a battlefield.
"It held up!"
"Unbelievable! What a great fort!"
"Now let's get to work!"

"I'll clear up around it!"
"I'll check the roof!"
"And I'll pick a bouquet!"

"Yum, this dandelion tea is delicious!"
"Even better than yesterday!"
"Tomorrow? Same time, same place?"

"Same time, same place!"

Marie Dorléans attended the School of Decorative Arts in Strasbourg, France, and has worked as a children's book illustrator since her graduation in 2010. Her previous book *Night Walk* won the Prix Landerneau, in the best children's book category.

Alyson Waters is a prize-winning translator of literary fiction from French to English. Her most recent translations for NYRB include the adult books Jean Giono's *A King Alone* and Emmanuel Bove's *Henri Duchemin and his Shadows* as well as the children's book *The Tiger Prince* by Chen Jiang Hong.